MY
Jolly Time
STORY BOOK

Brown Watson (Leicester) Ltd.
CHILDREN'S BOOK PUBLISHERS
55A, London Road, Leicester LE2 OPE

An Afternoon at the Fair

Janey and Jimmy decided that they would like to go to the fair, so they collected all the pennies and five pences from their piggy banks and set off. They bought two lollipops and sucking these they made their way to the merry-go-round.

Like all boys Jimmy wanted to ride a wild horse, so he picked the wildest looking horse and imagined he was in the Wild West. He shouted with glee as the horse bucked and kicked. "You had better be careful or you will fall off," said Janey.

When they got to the balloon man's stall he had just let off a whole lot of balloons for the balloon race. There were all sorts and sizes of gay balloons in many different shapes. Some of them had very funny faces, but the wind soon whisked them out of sight.

"All this fun makes one very hungry," said Jimmy as he saw the stall selling hot pancakes. "I would like one of those big round ones." Then when no one was looking he popped his fingers in the whipped cream and swallowed it in such a hurry that he almost took his fingers too.

When they could eat no more they went to the shooting gallery. "Take a good aim at the bullseye" said Janey. She was very proud of her brother because he was a very good shot, but she was even more proud when he won a nice prize.

Next they tried the swing boats, but they were quite frightened when they got up high and they huddled together. All the people below looked like little dolls, but although they were a little afraid, they enjoyed the ride immensely.

"I'm glad we have got back to earth again," said Janey. "Let's have a drink to recover from the ride." When they had finished their nice cool drink they decided

to try the bumper cars. "I'll drive," said Janey, gleefully.

"Oh no! not a woman driver," said Jimmy, but Janey was very good and only hit another car once or twice. This doesn't really matter because the bumper cars are made to bump. After this they both went home feeling very happy, but very tired.

Charlie and Charlotte go to Town

Children who live in big cities often dream of visiting a farm and likewise children who live on farms often want to see big cities. For this reason Farmer John told his children, Charlie and Charlotte that they could visit the city if they did well in their examinations.

Their first trip by train was so exciting that they were in the city before they knew it. First of all they went to visit the zoo. Charlie thought that the horses were wearing pyjamas until Charlotte told him they were Zebras.

In the city squares they discovered that the pigeons were all very tame, and when they bought some nuts, the pigeons flocked to them. They were so tame that one perched on Charlotte's head and another on Charlie's hand. They both agreed that this was very exciting.

"Everything in the country seems much smaller than it is in the town," remarked Charlotte, who was thrilled by the churches and towers. "Just look at the cross on top of that cathedral," cried Charlie, "it almost touches the sky."

When it was tea time both the children went and had tea by the sea and you can imagine their excitement when a coaster sailed into the port. "It must be wonderful

to be a sailor," said Charlie dreamily. "Let's ask daddy if we can go on a sailing trip next holiday."

"Well! we can't stop here all day," said Charlotte. "We must hurry if we don't want to miss the parade. Listen, I can hear the drums already." — "Just look at the soldiers," cried Charlie excitedly, "they are

as stiff as pokers, and what beautiful straight rows they march in."

After the parade the children went to a circus. They were very surprised at the wonderful tricks that the animals could perform. "I think it would be great fun to teach our farm animals to perform tricks like that," remarked Charlie.

Before going home they went to a fancy dress ball. They dressed up as a Spanish couple, and imagine their surprise when they won first prize. The prize was a beautiful red car and driving home in it made a marvellous end to a fabulous day.

KING BIMBO AND THE ROBBERS

"Good morning, your Majesty! What a lovely day," said the Lord Chancellor, whose name was Ponk.

"Is it?" came a muffled voice from the bed.

"Of course, Sire! Can't you see...."

"How can I see when my head's tucked under the bedclothes?"

"Come, come, Sire! I think it would do your Majesty good to go for a nice drive through the forest," said Ponk, rubbing his hands.

The bedclothes shot into the air, and King Bimbo sat up with a jerk.

"I know why you want to get rid of me," he said. "It's so that you can play a game of tiddly-winks with the others."

"But, Sire...."

"Don't deny it!" Bimbo went on. "Nobody ever asks me to play. But I know why. It's because I always win."

The Lord Chancellor heaved a sigh. "Whatever you say, your Majesty. Now here is your breakfast," and he placed a bowl of steaming porridge on the bed, and then left the room.

When King Bimbo had dressed himself, he went down to the stables to see if the coach was ready. The grooms were nowhere to be found so he had to harness the horses himself.

"I always have to do things myself," he grumbled.

Then he had to hunt high and low to find the coachman. At last they were ready, and away they went. They followed the road that wound its way through the forest. Suddenly, the coach began to slow down, so Bimbo poked his head out of the window and demanded to know the reason.

"There are some people in front waving, Sire," the coachman told him.

"What of it?" grunted Bimbo. "I suppose they can wave to their own king, can't they? You don't have to stop. I'm not going to make a speech."

But the coach did stop, and a crowd of faces appeared at the window. Then someone called out: "Give us a lift! We are footsore and weary. Thank you kindly!" And before Bimbo could say a word, the door was pulled open and they all began climbing in. It was a proper scramble. Bimbo himself was pushed across to the

other side of the coach, and he bumped
up against the door. It swung open and
he fell into the road.

By the time he had recovered his wits
the coach was some distance away. He

yelled and shouted and shook his fists in the air, but the coach just rolled on out of sight.

"This — this is an outrage!" he stormed. "It's highway robbery! Stealing my coach and leaving me to walk."

His words were uttered in vain, of course, and he had to begin the long trudge back to the palace. Not that he went that far, for a number of fierce looking men suddenly sprang out from behind the trees.

"Oh, dear!" said Bimbo nervously.

The leader of the gang eyed him up and down.

"Who are you?" he snarled.

"I—I am the k-k-king," Bimbo stammered.

"Did you hear that, men?" cried the robber chief. "We should get a good price for him."

"P-price!" gulped Bimbo. "Am-am I to be s-sold?"

"Aye! We're going to hold you to ransom," chuckled the robber.

They took him back with them to their camp in the forest, and he was forced to spend the night curled up in front of a fire. Early next morning one of the men gave him a nudge.

"I think I will have breakfast in bed this morning," Bimbo mumbled in his sleep.

"What's that?"

Bimbo opened his eyes with a start and looked about him. When he saw that he was still in the robber camp, he groaned.

"Hurry up there! We want some food," growled the robber.

Poor Bimbo was made to prepare the meal for them, but it took him a long time to do it. He tried hard the while to think of some way of making his escape, and all at once an idea came to him.

"Why didn't I think of that before?" he murmured to himself. Then he went up to the robber leader and said: "If you take me safely back to the palace, I'll give you all the money that's in the Royal Money-Box."

The man looked at him craftily. "What kind of a trick is this?" he roared.

"It's no trick! I mean it — honest!" said Bimbo.

For a while the robbers spoke to each other in whispers, then the leader said that he would take Bimbo back himself. It took them a long time to reach the palace as they had to walk all the way, and poor Bimbo's feet ached terribly.

"Your Majesty!" cried Ponk, when he saw them come through the gates. "We thought we'd lost you."

"Well, you haven't! Now fetch the Royal Money-Box," ordered Bimbo.

The Lord Chancellor hurried away and brought it back.

"How much is there in it?" Bimbo asked.

"Ninepence, Sire!"

"Give it to this man. He's earned it," said Bimbo.

"Is that all there is?" the robber exclaimed, his eyes almost popping out of his head.

"That's all!"

"Well, robber though I am, I wouldn't think of taking your last few coppers. Here! You'd better have this," and he dropped a florin into the box.

"Thank you very much," beamed Bimbo. "What a nice gentleman. You must call again."

And the robber chief said that he would.

THE END

TIM THE TALKATIVE TAILOR

"Ah! This should mean some work for me," cried Tim the Tailor, as he stared at the big poster outside the Fairytown Hall. The poster read:-

GRAND FAIRY BALL
The Fairy Queen will present a prize of 1,000 Acorns to the person wearing the most beautiful and unusual costume. All the people of Fairytown are invited to attend.

Ideas raced through his head.

"I shall be able to make myself the richest tailor in the whole of Fairyland," he thought to himself. "No other tailor will be able to make a costume as good as mine."

Tim turned away and walked down the street with a gleam in his little brown eyes. Even before he had a customer he was thinking of the splendid costume he would make.

"I'll make only one," he muttered to himself. "I'll give all my time to it, and when it wins the first prize people will come to me from all over Fairyland for their clothes."

By the time he reached the door of his little house he had made wonderful plans for the future. The people who would come to him when the prize was won would want far more suits than he could ever make. So he would need lots of other tailors to help him. Then he would make so much money.

"Hello."

Tim was opening the front door when he

heard the voice at his side. He turned and saw Flip, the friendly Imp.

"I've got a job for you," said Flip, with a merry smile that stretched right across his chubby face.

"Oh! Then you'd better come in," replied

Tim, as he led the way into his tiny parlour.

"Look at these," cried Flip, as he drew his hand out of his pocket.

"How beautiful," answered Tim, eagerly, as he gazed at the small berries held before him. Their colour was golden red like the morning sun.

"Yes," cried Flip, "I have thousands of them, and no one else has any. They are magic berries planted by a good fairy at the end of our garden."

"I like them very much," said Tim. "But what do you want me to do with them?"

"I want you to make me a costume out of them for the Fairy Ball," replied Flip, his eyes gleaming with excitement.

Tim brought his fingers together with a click. "That's a good idea," he cried. "I'll make it the finest costume that's ever been seen in Fairyland."

"Good," gasped Flip. "You see, I need the prize so much. Our landlord wants to turn my mother and me out of our cottage. But if I win the prize I can buy the cottage."

"Don't worry," said Tim. "With my costume you'll win."

Then Flip remembered that people said Tim could not keep a secret. "Remember," he stated, "No one must know what I'm going to wear. If they expect to see me in red berries, my costume won't be unusual and I'll never win."

"I'll tell no one," promised Tim.

And Tim really meant what he said. But he was so happy at the thought of making the winning costume that he could not resist doing a little boasting. Of course, he

did not describe the costume he was making, but hinted that the one he was making would be finer than any other.

Now Bink the Barber heard of Tim's boast. Bink was rather a mean fellow and meant to win the Fairy Queen's prize himself. So as soon as he heard of this boast he decided to find out what sort of a costume Tim was making.

So, for two days, he watched from his front window the people who went into Tim's shop. He saw Flip enter each day with a little box under his arm. His wicked eyes glistened. He must find out more about the boxes.

On the third day he watched from behind the hedge around Flip's cottage. In the afternoon he saw Flip fill a little box with red berries and then walk off to Tim's shop. Bink followed and then waited outside the shop until Flip came out once more. Then he crossed the road and entered the shop.

"Hello," he said, as he faced Tim over the little counter, "I wonder if you could make me a costume for the Fairy Ball?"

As he asked the question he glanced all round in search of the box Flip had brought. But Tim had taken the box into his house where no one could see him working.

"I'm afraid I can't," replied Tim.

"I suppose you're making one for someone else," said Bink.

"Well, yes, I am," admitted Tim.

"What's it like?" asked Bink.

"It'll be the finest costume ever seen," boasted Tim. "I can't tell you any more."

"Hmm," murmured Bink. "It's no use my trying if you're making a costume for someone else. You're the best tailor in Fairyland."

Of course, Bink was not telling the truth. He had another tailor already making his costume for him. But he hoped by talking in this manner to persuade Tim to give away his secret.

"Do you really think that?" gasped Tim, in delight.

"Of course. No one can really work with red colours except you," Bink went on remembering the berries in Flip's garden. "If you make a red costume it's certain to win the first prize."

"Oh!" cried Tim, jumping with glee. "That's marvellous. I'll let you into a secret. It will be red just like the rising sun."

Bink's little eyes gleamed wickedly. He had found out what he wanted to know.

"Good luck, then," he said, as he walked out of the shop.

But as soon as he reached the street he told everyone that Flip was going to wear a costume of red berries. Even the Elf who was to judge the costumes at the Ball heard and said: "There's nothing unusual about red berries."

Tim was busily working, so he did not know what was happening. But that evening Flip called on him and told him that everyone knew all about the costume.

"You nasty thing," cried Flip. "Everybody knows what I'm going to wear at the Ball, and only you could have told them. I should have known you couldn't keep a secret."

"I never —" began Tim.

Then he remembered his talk with Bink.

"It was that wicked barber," he cried.

But Flip took no notice of him.

"I shall never win the prize now," he wailed. "My costume will never be unusual if everyone knows what it's like. And my mother and I will be turned out of our cottage. Oh dear!"

With that he walked away with big tears running down his cheeks.

Tim looked after him feeling very unhappy. Yes, he, Tim, was to blame for it all. If he had not boasted about the costume in the first place Bink would never have wanted to find out what he was making.

He closed the front door and sat down before his little fireplace. It would be his fault if Flip and his mother were turned out of their cottage. He had to do something. But the Ball was to be held tomorrow night. Perhaps a little walk in the quiet wood would help him to think.

So he went out and walked to the little wood, where he sat down on a seat between the trees. He tried to think out a new and unusual costume for Flip. But he could think of nothing good enough, and when night came with the moon peeping through

the trees he still sat in the same place.

"I must think of something to save poor Flip," he moaned, with a big tear in the corner of each eye.

It was then he heard the voice at his side. He turned and saw the Silver Fairy.

"I think you're cured," said the Fairy, "so I'll help you to make a new costume for poor Flip."

"Oh! Will you really, good fairy?" cried Tim, jumping to his feet.

"I will," answered the Fairy. "But you must first promise to remember that each time you gossip you may break someone's heart."

"I will never gossip again," promised Tim.

Then he went to his little house. The Fairy summoned a hundred spiders, who spun a glorious golden thread, and a thousand butterflies who lent their glistening wings.

Tim worked hard all through the night

and for most of the next day. An hour before the Ball was due to begin the costume was finished. He wrapped it up and ran to Flip's house.

"What do you want?" asked Flip, as he opened the door.

"Look," cried Tim, as he opened his parcel. Flip's eyes opened wide as he saw

the glittering costume.

"It's wonderful!" he cried.

"Put it on," said Tim, "and go to the Ball."

With a happy smile on his chubby face Flip obeyed. And later his splendid costume won him First Prize, so that he was able to buy his cottage.

As for Tim, he soon had hundreds of new customers. His reputation had spread throughout Fairyland and customers came from all over the fairy world. By now he had learnt his lesson and he didn't gossip anymore, so he was able to keep all his customers.

As it happened the Fairy Queen had been very impressed with Flip's Costume at the ball, and very soon Tim was able to put up a large notice outside his shop which read:

TIM
by appointment
tailor to
HER MAJESTY
THE FAIRY QUEEN

Very soon he was the most famous and the richest tailor in all the land.

THE END

ALEC AND THE LITTLE MAN

Alec had been a naughty boy all day. First of all he would not clean his teeth. Mummy had been cross about that, and, in the end, she had made him do it. He was late for school, though, because of the fuss.

Then he would not eat his parsnip for dinner.

"Nasty-tasting stuff!" he said, and again Mummy was cross. There were lots of other things that day, too, It was muddy, and he would not wipe his boots. Then Mummy wanted some shopping done, and Alec wanted to be paid a penny for doing it.

"No," Mummy said, "being a Scout, you must do some good deeds without being paid for them."

Alec wanted to be paid. He pouted and said he would not go, then.

This time Mummy was really cross — more cross than he had ever seen her.

"I believe you are being trying just because Daddy is away," she said. "You ought to be a help, but instead you have a little man on your shoulder. Now you just go upstairs and get into bed, and stay there till the man has gone."

Slowly Alec dragged his feet upstairs, kicking the stair rods at every step.

He dared not disobey Mummy when she looked so fierce. No, not fierce exactly.... anyway he had to do what she said now.

"Ha, ha! Lovely night for going to bed." Alec jumped as a squeaky voice spoke in his ear. He looked round and saw a tiny man perched on his shoulder.

He was a funny, little man, and he had a tall, pointed hat and long, pointed shoes.

His nose was turned up and his eyes smiling with mischief.

'Get into bed with your dirty boots on," said the little man. "Your mother just said, 'Get into bed.' She didn't say undress."

Alec sat down on the side of the bed and thought. He still felt cross, but he was not such a naughty boy as that!

"That would make Mummy more cross than ever." he said at last.

"Well, that's what you want to do, isn't it?

Alec shook his head, and perhaps he knocked the little man off his shoulder. Anyway, when Alec had taken off his boots, he looked round. The little man was perched on the end of the bed now.

He was looking cross, though, instead of smiling.

"If you are going to be a goody-goody, I'll have to go away. Just when I thought I was going to have a lot more fun, too," he said.

Alec stood looking at him. What an ugly little man he was.

"Do you always sit on my shoulder when I am naughty?" he asked. The little man chuckled.

"Oh yes, always," he said. "We have had lots of fun today, haven't we? And, of course, the longer I stay the worse you get. I tickle you with my long shoes and, hey presto, you get more and more cross."

"Oh!" Slowly Alec undressed and when he was in bed, looked down at the little man on his bed-rail.

"You are a nasty, ugly, little thing," he

cried. "Go away. I won't have you on my shoulder any more."

"All right. If you don't want me I shall have to go," he said sulkily. "I suppose you would rather have my brother, Goody Redjacket."

He kicked his long shoes in the air and started to turn a somersault backwards, and then, suddenly sitting on the hump made by his knees in the bed, Alec saw a dear little man.

This one was dressed in white satin trousers with a red jacket over a white shirt-front. Soft curls covered his head, and there were large white rosettes on his little red shoes.

Alec smiled.

"Hullo, Goody Redjacket," he said.

"How do you know my name?" asked the little man.

"Your brother told me," Alec replied, looking towards the bottom of the bed, but the little man was not there now.

"Oh, I see, so that is why you are in bed," said Goody Redjacket. "You have been a naughty boy."

Alec's face went red. It was very horrid to hear this little man say he had been a naughty boy like that, in a sad voice. He felt very guilty and very sorry.

"I am going to try to be good now," he said.

"That's right. Then I will help you," said Goody Redjacket, smiling cheerfully.

"Well, how do I start?" asked Alec.

"First of all you must call your mother and tell her you are sorry."

"But she was very cross," Alec told the little man.

"No, she was more sad than cross, really," said Goody. "She is sad because your Daddy has just gone abroad and she is sad because you have been naughty. She is sitting in her chair downstairs now, crying......"

"Crying?" echoed Alec. "Oh, poor Mummy! Would she stop if I said I would

be good?"

The little man nodded his head. "Call her and just see," he said.

"Mummy! Mummy!" called Alec at the top of his voice. He heard his mother's footsteps come slowly along the passage and up the stairs. She seemed a terribly long time coming, but at last she stood by the side of his bed.

"Well, Alec," she asked, "What did you want?"

Alec looked up at her. Yes, Goody Red-jacket had been right. Mummy's eyes were red, and there were still tears on her eye-lashes.

"I'm sorry about being naughty," he said, in a small voice, "and I won't be — ever — again."

Mummy smiled then, a twinkly smile, like Goody Redjacket's. She knelt down by the bed and ruffled his hair with her fingers. It was a nice feeling, and it was nicer than having Mummy cross.

"Mummy," he said solemnly, "I am going to be good for always, because the little man is such a horrid creature, and Goody Redjacket says he will help me, don't you Goody Redjacket?" Alec looked towards where he had last seen the little man, but he had vanished.

"Oh, he's gone," he cried in disappointment.

"Never mind, he'll stay close to you all the time you are good, even though you cannot see him," Mummy said, "and he is much better than the little man, I know."

Alec smiled.

"Do you think there is time to get to the shops before they close?" he asked, and Mummy nodded. "Yes, I think so, just about, if you hurry," she said.

THE END

CHRISTMAS EVE

It was Christmas Eve! "Tick-tock, Tick-tock," said the Grandfather Clock on the stairs. "Tick-tick," went the clock on the mantelpiece. Joan was lying awake in bed, waiting for Father Christmas. She was so excited, but was soon asleep and off to "Dreamland." She could in her dream still hear the tick-tock, tick-tock of the big clock and the tick-tick of the little clock.

Then she saw the little clock dance a jig, and look just like a little boy. "Come out Grandfather!" he cried, "It's Christmas Eve; where shall we go tonight?" Grandfather hobbled out of the big case and stood beside the little clock-boy.

"I am so tired," said Tick-tick.

"So am I," answered Tick-tock, "But shall we go and call on Father Christmas? He asked us to go soon. Shall we take Joan too? She has been a good little girl today!" Tick-tock poked Joan, and she sleepily rubbed her eyes. In front of her she saw two funny little men.

"Come with us," said Tick-tick.

"Who are you?" asked Joan, looking very surprised.

"We're Tick-tick and Tick-tock, and Father Christmas asked us to visit him. We thought you would like to come too," they answered.

"Yes, please! I would," cried Joan, clapping her hands.

They took Joan's hand and opened the door of Grandfather Tick-tock's home. Inside were some little stairs. Soon they came to the bottom, where there, in a large garden, was a beautiful big house with many windows. Joan, Tick-tick and Tick-tock walked up the drive and knocked at the door. Waiting at the front door was Father Christmas's sleigh with four reindeers all ready.

"Do you think he is too busy to see us?" enquired Joan.

"I don't expect so," answered Tick-tock as the door opened.

"Please can we see Father Christmas?"

"Come in," said the Snow Fairy, who lives with Father Christmas, "He is rather busy, but perhaps you can help to pack the toys."

"We would love to," all three replied. They all went into a big room, where Father Christmas was busy packing all the toys. It looked like the Bazaar where

Mother had taken Joan yesterday.

"Come along," he said, "I am very busy; you may help me if you like." So Joan, Tick-tick and Tick-tock began to pack the toys. There were dolls and balls, trains and aeroplanes, some for boys and some for girls.

"Some are for little boys and girls who have no Mummies and Daddies," said Father Christmas. Soon they had finished, and they all helped to carry the toys to the sleigh.

"Would you all like to come with me?"

"Please!" answered Joan.

In they all jumped, and off they went over the hills and far away through the forest into the town among the chimney pots. The sleigh stopped and in they crept; Father Christmas by the chimney.

"Look!" said Joan.

"S'sh," said Tick-tock, "You'll wake up the babies."

In white little beds lay boys and girls dreaming of Santa Claus. On every bed hung a little stocking. Father Christmas brought his sack into the middle of the room.

"Come, Joan," he said, "You may tell me what little girls like, and you, Tick-tick, what little boys like."

Soon there were no toys left in the sack, and on tip-toe Father Christmas and his helpers crept back to the sleigh.

They called at lots of houses, and each time Father Christmas came back with an empty sack. Soon there were only a few toys left.

"Here you are back home," said Father Christmas, stopping the sleigh. "Now run

along to Sleepyland, and when you are asleep I am coming to fill your stocking with a beautiful surprise."

"Thank you for letting me help!" replied Joan as she ran into her house.

"Wake up! sleepy-head," called mother, "look what Father Christmas has brought you."

"I have been helping him," answered Joan, "and I will tell you all about it after breakfast."

THE END.

THE STONE WHO WOULD GO A'ROLLING

There was once a stone who wanted to go a'rolling. "You will never be covered with beautiful moss like me unless you keep in one place," said Grandmother Stone severely.

"I don't want to keep in one place, nor to be covered with moss," said the stone. "I want to see the world." "You see plenty of the world here. John Ploughman passes every evening, and yesterday three ducks crossed the road."

"There's more in the world than John Ploughman and three ducks," replied the stone. "Master Rook told me when he perched on you yesterday."

"Tiresome creature," cried Grandmother Stone, "upsetting young stones, and putting ideas into them."

"I asked the rook what that humming noise was that we can hear, much louder than bees, and he said, 'Motors.' I want to go to the big road and see them."

"I have done without motors — whatever they are — all my life," said Grandmother Stone, "so why can't you?" And she went to sleep. But the stone tingled to get away. The next day, who should come along but a little girl, and she stopped just in front of Grandmother Stone and the young one.

"Hullo, stone," she said, poking him with her foot. "You must be tired of sticking in one place all the time. I'll

take you with me."

The stone shivered with delight as he was picked up. "Good-bye, Grandmother, I'm going to see the world," he shouted in glee.

The little girl hugged the stone in her soft hand and made him feel warm, reminding him of the sun shining on him.

When they reached the high road, she carried him some little way, then stopped and put him down at the edge of the path. "There," she said, "now you can watch the motors go by, and not get under them."

Just what the stone wanted! He was pleased.

After a time, when he had grown used to the rushing and humming and hooting, he began to want another change.

Luckily for him it came. Two boys came down the road and looked up at the big tree close by.

"I say, Tommy," said one. "Conkers! Where's a stone?"

"Here you are," said the other, picking up the stone, and the next thing he knew he was whizzing up into the air.

Bang! He had hit a chestnut.

"Whatever are you doing?" cried the

chestnut indignantly, as he and the stone fell to the ground together.

"It's not my fault," said the stone. Up he went again. Bang! Down came another chestnut. "This is splendid," cried the stone. "I don't mind how many chestnuts I hit." "But we do," answered the chestnuts, shaking with anger. "I can't help it," said the stone, "I'm seeing the world." Soon the boy's pockets were full, so they dropped the stone and went away.

"I wonder what will happen to me next," thought the stone. "It was glorious, soaring up into the air like a bird; I wish I could tell Master Rook."

Night came on. He lay by the wayside, wet with dew, and the great head-lights from the passing motors made him sparkle and glow. It was as thrilling as when he was flung into the air.

He was impatient for new adventures, but nothing further happened until the

boy who scared away rooks for Farmer
Giles was going home to his tea.

As he went slouching along, his toe
happened to hit against the stone, so he
went on kicking it in front of him until
he reached his mother's cottage. Then he
picked up the stone and threw it at a
sparrow. Fortunately the boy was a very
bad shot, and the sparrow flew away with
a cheeky flirt of his tail.

"I don't like being kicked," thought
the stone, "but it has brought me a little

further on my way, and there is certainly more to be seen in the world than John Ploughman and three ducks."

A tramp picked him up the next day to knock down a nail in his broken boot, and, not noticing what he was doing, he slipped the stone into the pocket of his extremely shabby coat. Presently, feeling something in his pocket, he pulled it out, thinking it was a piece of cheese. "Didn't know I had any left," he said. But when he found it was only the stone he flung it away in disgust.

The stone fell right on top of a heap of stones, put there for mending the roads.

A chorus of stony voices greeted the newcomer. "Hallo, who are you?" "You're not a bit like us." "You are so flat and smooth."

The stone looked at his new companions. "You seem all sharp points," he said. "I am decidedly better-looking than you." "Ah-ah," they all shouted. "You wait until the stonebreaker comes along. He will soon spoil your pretty smoothness." "How?" asked the stone. "He hits with a hammer and breaks us even smaller than we are."

"But why does he do that?" asked the stone.

"Because we are all packed into a worn out part of the road, and then a great black monster comes rolling over us and crushes us down, till we aren't stones any longer, but just part of the road."

"Well that's something anyhow," said the stone cheerfully.

"You think that? You won't feel quite so jolly about it when it is really hap-

pening," they told him. "Here comes the stonebreaker."

A man sat down on the heap. He was in his shirt-sleeves and was carrying a special kind of hammer.

He put on a pair of spectacles, took up a stone and hit it sharply with his hammer.

The young stone saw sparks fly from it.

Soon it broke in two, and the man picked up another, and again sparks flew. "I wonder if it hurts very much," thought the stone. "I like to see the sparks. Can there be sparks in me too?"

Another countryman passing called out "Good-day, Roadmender."

"Roadmender, that is a much more pleasant name than 'Stonebreaker'," thought the stone. "And it is we stones that mend the road. I'd rather do that than collect moss on me and never do a thing."

But after all he was not to help in mending the road. When the roadmender picked him up, he turned him over. "You're not a

flint," he said, "My little chap would like you." So instead of breaking him up the roadmender stuffed him into his pocket to take home.

The roadmender's cottage stood at the cross-roads, and a small boy was playing in front of it.

"Hey, sonny," said his father, "I've brought you something," and he took out the stone.

"Eh, Dad, what a beauty," cried the boy.

"So I'm a beauty, am I, I wish Grandmother Stone could know that." But he soon had the conceit taken out of him. The boy put him on the shelf, where he saw a lump of green glass, a bit of agate, several sea-shells, a pine cone, and a wonderful object — a ship in a bottle. They all began asking him what business he had among them. He was nothing but a plain stone.

"The boy called me a beauty," replied the stone. But they all laughed at him.

However, the laugh was on his side the next day, for the small boy took him to an old sailor.

The sailor pulled out his knife and deeply scratched a lovely little ship on the stone's smooth surface.

The stone knew what was happening by what the boy and the sailor said to each other. "A ship," he thought, "like the one in the bottle. This is better than moss. Now I shall be as good as those other proud things. What an interesting place the world is. I knew there was more in it than John Ploughman and three ducks."

THE END

TEN LITTLE BOYS

Once upon a time there were ten little Chinese boys. They wore little round hats and lived close to the big rice fields, where hundreds of rice plants grow in the shallow mushy water. One day they were out taking a walk, and as the sun was shining, each one of them carried a parasol. Now close to the house of Wang Sang, the horse merchant, is a deep well and when the little Chinese boys reached it they suddenly realized they were all very thirsty.

One said: "Shall we drink some water from Wang Sang's well?" They all agreed and one lowered the pail into the well; another one was just going to pull it up again when......

Whoops! he leaned over just a little bit too far and splash, in he fell. The others all screamed: "Help! Help!," in Chinese of course. Luckily Wang Sang was at home and he came running up in his brightly coloured slippers. He grabbed a long pole and thrust it down the well and fished the little Chinaman out of the water. He was the first one to have a narrow escape.

They made a very deep bow to Wang Sang and shuffled off. Do you know the path, that runs along the mountain side? Well, it's a very dangerous path! in parts it runs very close to the edge and if you aren't very careful, you can fall down into the deep valley below.

One of the boys spotted a beautiful red

flower growing just below the path. "Look a lovely red flower," he cried, "I'm going to pick it!" "No, no, don't be silly," said

the others, "once you fall it's too late!" He refused to listen and leaned over the edge to reach the flower and......

Need I tell you? Yes, he lost his balance and fell over the side. Down he tumbled, turning head over heels in mid-air as he went. It would only be a matter of seconds now, and he would crash into the valley below.

"Oh!!!" screamed the others and they all put their hands before their eyes.

Now along the rugged mountain side there is a big thick branch jutting out, and in this branch a big black crow had made his nest. "Hello," thought the crow as he saw the little Chinese boy come tumbling down, "that little fool's going to fall right on top of my head, if I don't look out," and he spread out his wings and flew off.

This little Chinese fell with a bump right into the Crow's nest. It was certainly a nice soft place to fall, and he didn't hurt himself a bit. He took a good look round: wondering where he was. He peeped over the side down into the valley a long, long way beneath him, then he looked up and saw nine little Chinese heads peering over the top. How was he going to get back again.

Luckily just at that moment fisherman Te Ping came trotting along. He looked over the side and quickly fastened a rope on to his basket of fish. He lowered it down and when he reached the nest in climbed the little Chinaman, and fisherman Te Ping pulled him up again.

Now there were eight little Chinamen to whom nothing had yet happened.

They thanked the fisherman and made their way to the forest. Now in this forest lived a huge tiger who thought to himself, "I could just fancy one of those fat little Chinese boys," and he sprang from behind a tree and grabbed one. The others ran off screaming with fright.

They rushed to the big strong game hunter Chang Ho and asked for his help.

Chang Ho grabbed his bow and arrow, and slapping himself three times on his hairy chest, made his way to the forest. Through the thick shrubbery he crept without making a sound. Spotting the tiger, he aimed his bow and arrow and Ping!! he hit the tiger first times.

The little Chinaman was free. Chang Ho then drew his knife and skinned the tiger.

The huntsman shouldered the Chinese boy and brought him back again to his brothers. The tiger's skin he took to the village and the villagers cheered him, they were all so relieved to see that the huge tiger had been killed.

This was number three to be rescued from an unhappy end.

Now there were seven of them to whom nothing had happened! But as you know there are crocodiles who live in the river and very often eat people, and as the boys are walking along the riverside a huge crocodile snatched at one of the little boys but luckily for him he was only caught by his trousers.

The crocodile thought to himself: "I'll take this nice little fat one over to the other side and have a good meal." He dragged the poor little fellow through the water to the other side. But who was sitting there on a flat stone sunning himself? Father Wong. When he saw the crocodile he began hitting him with a big stick until the crocodile had no choice but to let go of the little Chinese boy.

"Thank you," said the little Chinaman, "Thank you very much indeed." Now there were six of them to whom nothing had happened yet!

Now one of the little Chinese boys was standing on the other side of the river and he called out to the others. "Hallo there, hallo there." One of the other brothers climbed into a little red boat intending to row over to the other side to fetch his brother, but unfortunately the boat which belonged to Schoolmaster Kim Lie was leaking very badly.

The little boy was rowing with all his might, but when half way across the river the boat began to sink. The poor little chap screamed for help and luckily drifted towards the big round bridge which crossed the river.

Three men were standing on the bridge and when they heard the screams, they looked down into the river. All they could see was a little round hat floating on top

of the water. One of them jumped in and fished the little Chinaman out again. And so number five, too, had a lucky escape.

Now I wonder, have you any idea, what happened to number six? Well he was picked up by mistake by a wagoner on his way back from market. He had eight children of his own and he lifted up the little Chinaman and put him into the wagon with all the others. When he was about to pass through the main gates of the City he realized his mistake and pulled him out again and left him by the roadside. Now there were only four of them to whom nothing had happened!

And now for number seven. He completely lost his way and was much too shy to ask anybody to help him. Greengrocer Lolo Ting saw him wandering about, crying his eyes out. She gave him an orange and told him which way to go, and soon found his brothers again.

Now there were three to whom nothing had happened. I wonder if anything will happen to the remaining three.

On they shuffled, all ten of them, through the centre of the town. They bought a big kite with a very long tail.

They started to fly it on the big open square in front of the Palace. Higher and higher it went, the string became tighter and tighter and the little Chinaman who was holding it was nearly lifted off his feet. But he wouldn't let go and suddenly the wind gave a sharp tug at the string and whoops! up into the air went number eight.

The others cried out to him: "Don't leave go now or you will have a long way to fall." But he couldn't hang on any longer and he had to let go and down he came.

He landed in the palace gardens on top of a prize cabbage in the vegetable patch.

"What's that?" cried the gardeners: "why, it's a little boy sitting in a cabbage; catch him quick!"

The palace sentry came marching up, to see what was going on in the vegetable garden.

"I'll get him," he cried. But he was too late, the little Chinaman was through the gateway before you could say Jack Robinson.

"I won't stand for this," screamed the sentry. "I'll show them," and he took a flying leap and grabbed......yes the ninth little Chinese boy, who wasn't quite quick enough to scurry off like the others. He

was thrown into a dark cellar without food and water. Luckily the lock was old and rusty and he was able to open it and creep out softly.

Outside the sentry was keeping watch and when he saw his prisoner about to escape he was after him like a shot; he was close on the poor little fellow's heels when...... What was that? Music? and drums too? Yes! The Emperor of China was entering the town.

Now when his Majesty the Emperor drives through the town, the people in the streets have to kneel down with their noses in the sand and not lift their eyes until the Emperor has passed. The sentry got quite a shock when he saw the Emperor approaching and quickly ran back to his post. All ten little Chinese boys fell respectfully on to their knees and buried their noses in the sand. This was how number nine managed to escape.

And what happened to number ten? Well he was very inquisitive, as he had never in all his life seen the Emperor in person. The Emperor was passing, carried by his forty servants, and just at that very moment the tenth little Chinese boy opened one eye. The Emperor saw it immediately.

"What's that," he cried. "Who is it, may I ask, that has the audacity to open his eyes? Bring the scoundrel to me at once." A soldier grabbed him and brought him to the Emperor.

"Don't you know that it is forbidden to raise your eyes when the Emperor is passing?" The little chap nodded and began to cry softly.

"Don't let it happen again," said the Emperor, "and by the way you had better let me borrow your parasol as the sun is so hot it is burning my head."

The little chap was more than pleased to be able to oblige the mighty Emperor.

When the ten little Chinese boys eventually arrived home, their parents said: "So there you are, and what have you all been up to today? Plenty of mischief, I suppose!"

"Yes we have," said the ten little boys and they told their Mother and Father in turn what had happened to them.

When they had all quite finished Mother said: "Now I do know how you lost your parasols, but am very pleased to see you home safe and sound."

THE SEARCH FOR MRS WHITECOAT

Mr. Wolf is a very unkind and cruel animal who doesn't like the other animals, so Wendy was very surprised when he talked of a beautiful Mrs. Whitecoat. She asked a little bird who she was, but he had never heard of her, so she and Peter decided to find where Mrs. Whitecoat lived.

On their walk north they met a white fronted gazelle. "Are you Mrs. Whitecoat" asked Wendy? "No!" replied the gazelle rudely and went on eating blossoms off a tree. "Since he is so rude," said Peter crossly, "we had better ask someone more polite."

They went to the dark woods and they met Mr. Oohoo, the very wise, old owl. "Do you know of the beautiful Mrs. Whitecoat?" asked Wendy — "I am told that she lives far to the north where there is always snow on the ground," said the old owl wisely.

Before they had gone very far, they met an inquisitive kangeroo. "Are you looking for me — or perhaps for my little one." she added as an after thought, pointing to her pouch where the baby sat? "No, we are looking for Mrs. Whitecoat, but you are brown." said Peter.

Soon they had to cross a stream where the eager beaver was working busily. They stopped to help him for a while and the beaver was very grateful. "You are very kind," he said. "It is not often that people are so helpful. This work is very tiring."

When they had finished helping the beaver, they travelled on. All of a sudden a goat jumped across their path. "Get out of my way," he complained. "How can I practice for the jumping competition with you there." — "How rude some animals are," snorted Peter and walked on.

By now the children were a long way north and they met a kindly stag who told them that the path was very rough. "You will have to walk carefully if you do not want to hurt yourself" he told Wendy.

At last they reached the cold snowy lands. "You will find her in the pine forests," replied the brown bear when Wendy asked him where she could find Mrs. Whitecoat. When they found her they understood Mr. Wolf's enthusiasm, for she was a most beautiful Ermine.

PALACE TO LET

King Bimbo was just going to eat his slice of bread and jam when there was a knock at the door.

"Come in!" he snapped angrily.

The door opened and in walked Ponk, the Lord Chancellor.

"Please excuse me, Your Majesty —"

"What is it?" Bimbo snorted. "Why am I always disturbed in the middle of my breakfast? I've never known such a house for interruptions."

"Your Majesty, he's here again," the Lord Chancellor announced.

"Who's here again?"

"The rent collector, Sire."

"Oh!" King Bimbo twiddled his thumbs. "How much money have we in the Royal Money-box?" he asked.

"Fourpence, Sire."

"Dear me! Is that all?" Bimbo cried. "Are you sure you haven't made a mistake with your counting?"

"Well, Sire, there is a trifle extra —"

"How much?"

"One bent ha'penny, Sire."

"Stop quibbling! Stop quibbling!" cried Bimbo. "How much rent are we paying now?"

"None, Sire! We haven't paid any for weeks," replied Ponk.

"Well, how much do we pay when we do pay it?"

"One pound."

Bimbo was thoughtful for a moment.

"Why not tell him to call back again?" he suggested.

"I did, Sire," said Ponk. "But he said that unless you paid the rent this time, he would have you thrown out. He's already fixed a board on the gate with the words 'To Let' on it."

"Have me thrown out, indeed!" Bimbo stormed, jumping to his feet. "That's a nice way for anyone to speak of his Monarch. Pay the miserable man!"

But the Lord Chancellor shook his head. "What with?" he asked.

"Oh, dear! What are we to do?" Poor Bimbo wrung his hands in despair.

"I will try again to put him off till next week," Ponk said. "In the meantime perhaps your Majesty will be able to think of something."

"Yes, do that! Do anything! But put him off!"

Away went the Lord Chancellor, and King Bimbo was left alone to brood over his troubles. He was so terribly worried, that when dinner-time came round he hadn't even touched his pair of kippers. Neither did he eat his hard-boiled egg for tea. And later, when he went upstairs to bed, he tossed and turned all night long.

Early next morning the Lord Chancellor opened the door of the King's private chamber to see if there were any letters to post. He had a big surprise, for Bimbo was sitting on the throne reading the morning paper.

"Your Majesty is up very early this morning," he declared.

"Don't stand there gibbering! Come over and help me," said Bimbo sharply. "I've decided to get a job. That's the only way I shall be able to pay the rent."

"A j-job, Your Majesty?" Ponk exclaimed, looking very stupid.

"That's what I said! Someone will have to work," Bimbo replied.

But although they searched right through the paper they didn't find anything suitable. There was only one thing to be done, and Bimbo did it. Wheeling his bicycle out of the palace gates, he mounted it and rode away to the local employment offices. He would have used the royal coach, but he couldn't do that as he'd already pawned it together with the horses.

When he arrived there he was given a small green card on which was written the address where he was to go for a job.

"Well I never!" exclaimed Bimbo. "This card tells me to call at my own palace. I didn't know they wanted anyone there."

It also stated on the card that he was to apply at the side entrance, so, when he arrived back at the palace he did this, and knocked on the door. It was opened by the cook who took one look at him and then slammed the door in his face, with the words: "Not today, thank you!"

This made King Bimbo very angry, of course, and he rapped on the door again, much harder this time. After much haggling he was allowed to enter, and was taken before the person who wished to employ him.

Gazooks and odd bodkins! It was the Lord Chancellor himself.

"So you are the new man, Sire. I will pay you fifty pence a week," he said.

"How much do I pay you?" Bimbo asked.

"Seventy five pence — when I get it," was the reply.

"Let me see now," said Bimbo, counting on his fingers. "If I take the job I shall have to pay you twenty five pence a week."

"That's right," Ponk nodded.

"In that case I don't think I'm going to enjoy working for you," Bimbo said firmly.

"In fact, I shall go into retirement this very minute."

"What about the rent?" Ponk reminded him.

"We shall have to think of something else," said Bimbo.

"What about a jumble-sale?"

"Have we any jumbles?" asked Ponk.

King Bimbo shook his head. "I don't even know what they look like," he confessed. Then his face suddenly burst into smiles. "I know the very thing! We'll hold a

grand ball. And if we put up notices saying that the King commands all his subjects to attend, we should make quite a lot of money."

"An excellent idea," Ponk agreed.

And that is what they did. Everyone had a glorious time, and King Bimbo was the happiest one of all, for he knew that he would now be able to pay the rent and would not have to move out of the palace.

THE END

FLUFFY BALL AND HIS ADVENTURES

When you get to the dandelion meadow near the river on a mild sunny morning in summer, there's a chance of your catching sight of Fluffy. What a strange little chap he is, making his seat on one of the largest dandelions he can find, happily watching a very pretty and gaily coloured butterfly.

At first you think, Look! a ball of fluff
from one of the dandelions is being whirled
along the ground by the wind, but then
all at once you discover that the ball of
fluff has tiny legs and little arms with a
small head and a gaily coloured hat.

And if you were then to stretch out your
hand to grasp him, you would not succeed
in doing so. For he would start running,
and he runs jolly fast, much faster than
you can. But should you, however, be
faster than he and nearly catch up with

him, he would stretch out his arms and
fly.

It is no use you trying again, you won't
catch him, for the wind helps him too.
Fluffy and the wind are great friends.

One fine day Fluffy happened to find
a large bottle on the bank of the river,
which had been washed ashore. He quickly
got into it to find out what it might look
like inside. How cosy it was, to be sure.

This is lovely, he thought, I am sitting
in this beautiful crystal house and can see
through the glass windows at all the glorious
scenery. This is so much better than my
old house and it is so light and airy. "I
think I'll move in and make it my very
own house!"

"This is where I'm going to live from now
on," he cried. The wind was just resting

in one of the willow trees for it was very calm on that day. It said: "Fluffy, you mustn't do that, you mustn't go and live in the bottle. Stay in your own cosy little home. That bottle has been washed up by the river, and when the river rises again it will carry off the bottle. The bottle belongs to the river and if you use it as your home you may be carried away. It's very risky to go and live in that bottle."

But Fluffy would not listen to the wise wind. He adored his new transparent house. It was cosy, with plenty of light coming in through the large windows. And the walls were smooth and nicely rounded. "No, this is the house for me!" thought Fluffy.

Flutter, the fieldmouse, who is always in a hurry, he runs along and never looks where he is going and is always stumbling, said: "Good gracious, what's that I hear! Surely Fluffy doesn't want to go and live in that bottle! It would be dreadfully dangerous." As he said this he stumbled

over a stone and fell to the ground. Quickly he got up: "Good gracious me, good gracious!" he mumbled. "Why doesn't the Mayor clear away these stones? I'm in such a desperate hurry. Good gracious!"

The Mayor, a big fat water rat, just happened to be sitting on a large stone in the water combing his moustache and drying his ears.

He looked up slowly as he heard Flutter's remarks and cast a disdainful look at the field mouse. He was not going to take any notice but couldn't help replying his usual opening remarks, "Pah! Pah!" Then the Mayor stared again at the fieldmouse and shrugged his shoulders.

"Pah, pah!" he exclaimed with great dignity, "Pah! Pah!, as if it were a Mayors' duty to clear away the pebbles. There are plenty of more important things for him to do," and he slipped into the water and lay there rocking contentedly in the ripples.

"Fluffy!" he called out. "Fluffy! What's dangerous about the river, I should like to know? You just go and live in the bottle, I'll be there to help you when the river rises. The Mayor helps everybody. It is nonsense to say that the river is dangerous," said the Mayor, and then he fell asleep.

He took no further interest in Fluffy or Flutter and snored loudly in his sleep.

"Don't do it, Fluffy!" cried the Wind. But then a boat appeared on the river with the limply hanging sails which needed blowing out, and, swish! off went the Wind at full speed, to do his proper job. But Fluffy, even if he heard, took no notice at all of the Wind's advice.

That very same afternoon Fluffy moved

in. First of all he placed a layer of dandelion fluff in the bottle; after that, assisted by Hare and Mr. Rabbit, he carried in his little chair and table and the cupboard in which he stored his honey pots, his tins of pollen and little cans of dandelion milk.

He had no bed, he just slept on the floor on the fluffs. This was quite comfortable. The door consisted of a wooden stopper, and he fastened this with a neat piece of wire so that he was snug inside his new bottle home.

When everything was ready Fluffy politely thanked Hare and Mr. Rabbit who were out of doors resting in the grass: "Would you both like a nice glass of dandelion milk?"

"No thank you, Fluffy," said Mr. Rabbit, "I'm not very fond of dandelion milk, it's much too bitter for my taste."

The Mayor also came to have a look at what was going on. He stroked his moustache with an air of dignity and importance.

"Pah, pah!, very nice, very nice indeed, Fluffy pah, pah, you'll see, I, the Mayor help everybody."

"You haven't done a thing," shouted Hare and Mr. Rabbit. "You're sprawling all day long on your big bed, that's all you do," they said, making fun of him.

So Fluffy lived all through the summer in his bottle. All went well. The river flowed along taking no notice of him and Fluffy was very happy. Day after day he gathered more and more pollen and honey and dandelion milk, for when the winter came he wanted to have his cupboard well stored.

But one day it started raining. The rain tinkled on the bottle. It would not stop. It came down in torrents. And all that rain fell into the river, which got more full from day to day. Every day it came a bit closer to the bottle. Mayor Water Rat came to look.

"Pah, pah" he cried through the doorway as he peered in. "What a fine bright place your living in, Fluffy." "Will — will the river carry away my bottle?" asked Fluffy anxiously.

"Nonsense, nonsense, the Mayor helps everyone, Pah, pah!"

Fluffy stayed in his bottle. One morning the river, which had got fuller carried off the bottle. And what did Fluffy do in his fright?

He shouted and yelled, but no one could hear him from his corked bottle, sad to say. He wondered what was going to happen to him and he wished he had taken Wind's advice.

The river rocked the bottle, everything in it tumbled down and got all mixed up. The little table was upset, his little chair rolled over. Luckily the food cupboard did not topple over.

Poor little Fluffy, how frightened he was, how he wished he had never gone to live in the bottle. Again the bottle rocked and once more he fell to the floor.

It was a terrible experience and all because he had not taken his friend's advice about his new bottle home. Oh!

dear, Fluffy did feel so sorry for himself.

When Fluffy was floating past Mayor Water Rat's hole he thought: "Now the Mayor is sure to come and rescue me."

But Mayor Water Rat was sleeping soundly in his bed. Whatever was Fluffy to do? Nobody saw what a dreadful thing was happening to Fluffy and his bottle.

He felt that all his kind friends had forsaken him and he was so alone, floating in the swollen river.

No one? Oh, yes, somebody did. It was Flutter, the fieldmouse, who saw it. He had been kept awake by the rain and was just about to go and have a look at the spot where the bottle had been all the time.

"Good gracious, good gracious! I've certainly not got much time to spare, but I must go and see whether Fluffy is alright."

When Flutter reached the river he very soon saw the bottle had been carried along by the river, but was it not the bottle he saw drifting along?

He ran along the bank of the river. "Good gracious," he shouted. "There goes our Fluffy swimming along and there's no one to stop him. Something will have to be done and I have got so little time," and with that Flutter stumbled over a blade of grass and fell so awkwardly that he sprained his ankle and was unable to walk a step. So he wasn't much help to poor Fluffy!

"Help, help," shouted Flutter and then once again. "Help."

But no one heard him. No one? Oh yes, someone else did.

Croak, the Crow, who was flying to the field did. He came down and asked: "Whatever's the matter, Flutter?"

"I fell down and my foot aches dreadfully," replied Flutter. "But never mind that. Do go at once and help Fluffy, for Fluffy has been washed away in his bottle. We must help him, help him!"

"All right," said Croak, "I'll do my best for him! I do hope your poor foot will be better soon. I'm off now to rescue Fluffy! — get on my back Flutter!"

"Help him, we must," shouted Croak. Now Flutter scrambled on to Croak's back and off they flew.

Meanwhile Fluffy in his bottle was drifting away faster and ever faster. He was feeling frightfully sad and looking so worried.

He sat staring in front of him in his swaying house and thought: "Now I'll be carried by the river into the sea. There the big waves will smash my bottle to bits and I'll be drowned. Oh dear, whatever will become of me. Do, please, help me someone!"

Poor little Fluffy felt so terribly lonely in his bottle and it was now drifting at a much faster speed. If only he could make someone see the plight he was in and come to his rescue.

Now and then a fish came swimming up and peered through the glass of the bottle, how big and terrifying they seemed.

Fluffy nearly died of fright, "Thank goodness they cannot get in," he thought.

He began to cry. "If I'd only stayed in my warm hole."

The river paid no attention: it just flowed on.

A couple of children were standing on a bridge. They shouted to some friends.

"Look, a bottle, see which of you can hit it!" and they pelted it with pebbles. Luckily they did not hit Fluffy's bottle, although some of the stones narrowly missed his glass house.

Fluffy thought the stones were going to hit his bottle, but fortunately they fell in the water round him. How glad he was when he was out of the reach of the stones. He floated along the river knowing all the time the sea was getting nearer and nearer.

Whatever would happen to his bottle when it reached the big waves of the open sea! Fluffy dared not think about such a terrible thing happening.

He caught sight of the lighthouse in the sea, just when he was beginning to think that he would never get help. Then help came. There was Croak with Flutter on

his back and all the countless members of Croak's family. About a hundred pitch black crows were there all flying in perfect formation.

Whatever was that thing they were carrying along together? It was a bit of an old fishing net that they had chanced to find lying beside a fishing boat. They gently lowered it over the bottle. On seeing this, Fluffy began skipping about in his bottle with relief and great joy.

At last his friends had found him, and he was going to be saved. Hurrah! Hurrah!

Now the Crows caught up the bottle in the net, rose high up into the air and thus they rescued Fluffy.

And that's how Fluffy made the whole journey home — by air! He didn't want to be anywhere near water any more. He had finished with water and once he was out of his bottle house, he would see that it was resting on dry land.

Oh! how stupid he had been to ignore all his friend's kindly advice. He felt he really deserved all the awful things that were happening to him.

His bottle was then put down in the middle of the dandelion meadow. Then Fluffy pushed open the cork door.

"Hurrah," all the animals shouted. They had all been waiting there for his return.

"Hurrah! Fluffy is back!"

And who was that coming along there?

Mayor Water Rat, his big belly preceding him.

"Pah! so now we've got Fluffy back again, I've...."

"Oh" shouted all the animals in chorus: "now just listen to him. He did not do a thing. Nothing at all. All he did was to sleep. He, who promised to help Fluffy. Flutter was the only one who helped."

And with that they hoisted Flutter on to Croak's back and in procession they paraded all over the dandelion meadow.

Fluffy is very happy now he is well away from the river, and really loves his glass bottle home.

THE DOG'S NIGHTDRESS CASE

Last summer Trixie, her mother and their cocker spaniel, Dasher, spent six weeks in a pretty country cottage. The house-agent gave them a list called an "inventory," on which everything they would find in the cottage was neatly typed.

"Go through it carefully, Trixie," her mother told her, "because we must make quite sure that everything on it is in the cottage now. You see, if there is anything missing at the end, we shall be expected to replace it."

One of the things on the list was "Dog's nightdress-case," and the dog was a black cocker spaniel, almost exactly like Dasher, except that, of course, he was made of wool and had a Zipp fastener down his "middle," so that the nightdress could be pushed inside him and kept there!

"I expect the lady the cottage belongs to, left that by mistake," Trixie's mother said. "She has left us the cottage furnished, but a nightdress-case is not exactly 'furniture'! So I think we'll put it away. I shouldn't like anything to happen to it."

Even while she was speaking they heard a growl from Dasher. He had caught sight of the case on the white counterpane and thought, apparently, that it was a real dog. Another moment, and he would have had it between his bared teeth. But Trixie had seized it and was holding it as high above her head as her arms would stretch: which was higher than Dasher could jump, though he had several good tries!

How Trixie and her mother laughed. But her mother wasn't quite easy until the case was carefully shut away in a drawer in her bedroom.

Two days before they were due to leave the cottage, Trixie had her tenth birthday. When her mother asked her what she would

like, she answered promptly, "A dog's night-dress-case, please, if it doesn't cost too much, exactly like the one here. Of course it will be a bit awkward with Dasher at first. But when he knows that it isn't a real dog, he won't care!"

"Well, we had better go to town this afternoon and see if we can get it," her mother said. "It isn't your birthday until tomorrow, but I shall be busy then turning out and packing, and the agent is coming to check up the things on the inventory."

Although they went to shop after shop Where nightdress-cases are sold, and had Dasher with them as a "pattern," they couldn't get another like the one at the cottage. The nearest was a black and white fox terrier.

"I think I'll have that, mother, please," Trixie decided. "Perhaps he won't annoy Dasher as much as a spaniel like himself seems to do!"

So the fox-terrier case was packed up, paid for, and they all went home to the cottage.

You can picture the confusion next morning. Trixie's mother turned out everything belonging to herself and Trixie on to the floor by the big trunk, ready for packing. In the middle of it all the agent marched in.

He went solemnly through the inventory, putting a tick by each thing on it as he found it.

"Dog's nightdress-case?" he read out enquiringly.

"In mother's chest-of-drawers," Trixie announced promptly But when she went to look, all the drawers were empty.

"It's among my own things on the floor I expect, Trixie," her mother said.

"It isn't," Trixie told her, when she had had a good look.

The agent was growing impatient. "I remember the thing as it happens," he said. "It was a cocker spaniel, like your own little dog."

He strolled off into another room, giving Trixie a chance of whisper.

"It can't be far away, mother. I know what I'll do. I'll seize Dasher and hold him tightly in my arms, not too close to the old agent, who is short-sighted I'm sure, by the way he keeps blinking!"

The trick might have worked, because Trixie held Dasher so that he couldn't even move his head. But alas! he could bark — and he did — just at the moment when the agent was licking his pencil ready to put a tick by "Dog's nightdress-case" on his copy of the inventory!

"I'll be jiggered!" he cried, and for a

moment Trixie thought he was going to be terribly angry.

Then he laughed, and they all laughed. Even Dasher put on a "doggy" grin.

"You'll have to replace the case if it doesn't turn up, though," he warned them. "I'll give you until tomorrow."

When he had gone Trixie and her mother searched feverishly. But there was no sign of the case anywhere.

"Where's Dasher?" Trixie asked suddenly.

She ran off to look, afraid that he might
have slipped out of the garden after the
agent. But she found him by the fence at
the bottom, growling fiercely and shaking
something between his teeth — something
black and woolly that he once looked like
himself, but now —

"Oh dear, what shall we do?" Trixie
cried in dismay.

Her mother, who had arrived on the scene, replied, "I shall have to write to the lady the cottage belongs to and ask her where she bought it. If it's quite impossible to get another like it, perhaps she will be content with a fox-terrier case like yours."

Before she had time to change her mind, Trixie burst out, "She can have the one you gave me, mother. I — I'm sure you can't really afford another."

"Well, it will be difficult," her mother admitted. "There has been so much expense lately, but I don't like to take away what I gave you for your birthday."

"I still have Dasher," Trixie smiled bravely. "And naughty though he is, he is nicer than a nightdress-case dog — though, of course, he is awfully nice too!"

So was the lady the cottage belonged to. "It doesn't matter a bit about the case,"

she wrote back. "As a matter of fact I had forgotten it. So please give the new one to your little girl, as you intended. But this time, watch the real dog!"

You may be sure they did. But Dasher, after one look at the new case, stalked off with a contemptuous, air, as much as to say, "You don't have me the same way twice!"

THE END.